Concealed in the Spotlight

Nicholas W. Pellegrino

First Edition

Copyright © 2021, 2022, 2023, 2024, 2025 Nicholas W. Pellegrino

All rights reserved.

ISBN: 979-8-9874152-6-9

DEDICATION

To the occupational therapists, behavioral therapists, physicians, psychologists, social workers, and other healthcare professionals helping patients with Tourette syndrome. Thank you for everything you do.

DISCLAIMERS

Although this is a fictional story, it depicts real experiences that some patients with Tourette syndrome face daily, from camouflaging tics to confronting OCD-like symptoms.

Tourette syndrome varies from person to person. Not all experiences will match the one depicted in this story. For example, although Everly experiences occasional coprolalia (involuntary and repetitive use of obscene language) in this novelette, only a small subset of patients with Tourette's experience coprolalia. Although the depiction of Tourette's in this story was written from genuine experience and research, one should never assume that everyone with Tourette syndrome experiences it the exact same way that Everly Hawthorne does in this writing. That said, we hope this story gives you some insight into life with this rare condition, as well as life with hidden/camouflaged conditions in general.

Additionally, please note that Everly Hawthorne's research in this novelette is fictional. Her initial descriptions of neural networks are based in truth, but everything that she claims to have invented/discovered during her dissertation defense are fictional concepts, added for the sake of the story.

CONTENTS

1 | CATASTROPHE

"Sorry, it's not supposed to break like this," Everly whimpered, fumbling with a cheap plastic remote. Some uncooperating threads of her brown hair fell over her eyes as she frantically spammed the *next* button, desperately hoping the projected display would move beyond the title screen.

"We don't have all day, Miss Hawthorne," spat an elderly man—his scratchy voice reminiscent of nails streaking down a chalkboard.

Everly stole a nervous glance at the research committee. The old man, Dr. Peart, sat on the far right: his face contorted into a wild frown as he tapped the armrest of his chair impatiently. Two to the left sat Dr. Caruso, a tall and slender woman with an intimidating stare, holding her arms crossed over her chest. In the middle, Niko—or, rather, Dr. Velkov—sat with his head in his hands. His face was red with embarrassment, as he was forced to watch his first PhD student blunder her way through this sad excuse of a dissertation defense.

"What are you looking at us, for?" Dr. Peart spat, sticking a finger in his ear as he spoke. "You can't figure this out for yourself?"

"Honestly," Dr. Caruso huffed, "she expects us to grant her a doctorate in computer science, yet she's so inept with technology, she can't even get a simple presentation working! What a waste of time."

Everly felt a crushing weight grow in the pit of her stomach. She was losing these people before the presentation had even started.

"Now, what's she doing?" Dr. Peart asked with a start. "What? You're winking at me? Are you trying to flirt?"

"What? I'm not winking—" Everly started to reply, though she was cut off by the shrill voice of Dr. Caruso.

"Flirting? The girl looks like she's having a small stoke, Dr. Peart. That's such a pity," the woman crowed, "and at the ripe young age of 28, no less."

Everly touched her hands to her face, and realized what was happening. A tiny, imaginary string had latched onto her right upper eyelid, and was being jerked down by an invisible hand in a sudden motion, over-and-over. With each mighty tug of the string, her head naturally tilted to the right, and her right eye was momentarily forced to shut.

"I'm sorry… it's not like that," Everly apologized. She tried to rip the imaginary string off her eyelid, but her hand passed right through it.

"You're going to stop that now, if you want to continue with your presentation," Dr. Peart commanded.

"Agreed. I'm quite uncomfortable with this student, Niko," Dr. Caruso added. Everly's advisor grumbled something unintelligible in reply, and looked as if he wanted to melt out of existence.

"It's not his fault!" Everly defended. "It's just me; I have Tourette's. It's a neurological disorder. It means I don't have full control over my body sometimes." Everly tilted her head to the right and winked as she spoke, her sudden fit unwilling to subside.

"The movement you're seeing is called a tic. It's kind of like a coughing fit, or having the hiccups," Everly desperately explained. "It just occurs, and there's nothing I can do about it."

"That is *disgusting*," Dr. Peart spat.

"Dr. Velkov, did you know about this?" the stern Dr. Caruso cried out. "Why did you waste six years training a student that can't even function like a *normal* human being?"

"I am *repulsed*," Dr. Peart continued, his neck tightening as his face wrinkled with a sour look.

Everly rubbed at her eye, trying to mess up the imaginary string's tension. In response, the string suddenly pulled harder, forcing Everly to compress her neck in an unorthodox movement. The young researcher gritted her teeth, as the strain of this motion immediately formed a crick in her right shoulder.

"This is despicable. You're done! Get out," Dr. Peart shouted, raising his hands dismissively.

A large buildup of pressure suddenly formed in Everly's chest, pushing and scrambling toward her throat. As Everly tried to comprehend the dismissal Dr. Peart had just given, her head unconsciously bobbed forward, and a sharp whistle flew out from her mouth.

Like clockwork, her body immediately forced her to wink and click her teeth twice—after all, that's simply what needed to happen after a whistle occurred.

"Please, at least hear out my presentation first," Everly pleaded, tears welling up in her eyes. Another sharp whistle forced its way out from her throat—followed by two teeth clicks and a wink.

As if taking the competing tic as a challenge, the imaginary string attached to her eye started to tug with renewed rigor, forcing Everly to continue winking her eye with a frantic, irregular rhythm.

"That's it," Niko shouted, standing up and slamming his hands down on the committee's table. The middle-aged researcher kept his head bowed, unable or unwilling to make eye contact with Everly. "Didn't you hear him? You failed! *So, get the hell out of my life.*"

As those sharp words pierced her trembling ears, Everly felt an electric jolt shoot through her body. Her eyes snapped open, and she found herself staring at the bland, white-colored wall of her college apartment. She was lying sideways in her bed, under three layers of sheets, with a blanket wrapped tightly around her head and held taut over her mouth.

It was just a nightmare, Everly realized, breathing heavily into the blanket. Her body was drenched in sweat, and her heart was beating rapidly. *Just a bad dream. A tic dream, too. Those are the worst.*

Everly sat up, pushing the blanket off her head. As her breath caught up with her, she felt the invisible string form over her right eyelid. "Fuck you," she mumbled, attempting to pull on the string. Her hand went right through it, as if the string were a ghost. Her head tilted to the right, and she winked, letting out a small squeak from her throat as she did so.

Then with a whistle, two teeth clicks, and another wink, Everly slipped out of bed. She sauntered over to her nearby window, and pulled open the blinds. Outside, it looked to be the crack of dawn. Light snowflakes fell like feathers dancing in the sky, and the sheet-covered ground blinded her with reflected sunlight.

Way too early to get up, she thought, rubbing her eyes. With her room now flushed in morning sunlight, Everly turned around and scanned her surroundings. *I'd better make sure nothing changed around here while I was asleep,* she decided.

A printed copy of her dissertation was still sitting loose on her bed, next to the crumped blanket she'd just tossed aside. By the bedroom door, her pair of black business shoes remained perfectly perpendicular to the wall. Her small cellphone was still crammed inside the right shoe, connected to a nearby wall outlet via a yellowed charging cable.

Next to her shoes, a button up shirt and dress pants sat perfectly flattened out along her wooden boot bench. Above those, her matching leather purse hung from a hook in the wall. Indeed, Everly had everything ready-to-go for her dissertation defense this afternoon.

Everly tightened her nightgown, then walked into the bathroom connected to her bedroom. She turned on the light, and studied her reflection in the mirror.

Bland. Boring. Uninspired, she thought. Her face was about as common as they come: light skin, brown eyes, and brown hair. She did have some freckles going for her, but they seemed hardly visible in the winter.

The way I look won't matter once I have a PhD, though, she thought, poking the squishy skin on her cheek. *They don't print your picture in a research paper. They list your name, email, credentials, and where you work. Simple as that. Everyone's in the same field, and the quality of your research is the only way to stand out.*

Everly re-entered her bedroom, and stared at the sheets of dissertation jumbled together on her bed. *Six publications. This is just the beginning for me... assuming nothing goes wrong during my dissertation defense, that is.*

For now, I'd better get some more sleep, Everly mused, as she walked up to the bedroom door and jiggled the doorknob.

Still locked, she observed. She attempted to turn the lock even further into the locked position, then jiggled the doorknob again. *Good,* she thought.

The 28-year-old researcher took a step back from the door, and turned to face her bed. *Unless... what if the door*

somehow unlocked itself when I jiggled the knob from the inside?
she pondered. *If that happened, then it's not locked anymore. If
someone broke into my apartment, they could walk into my
bedroom without a second thought; it's critical to have the
bedroom door locked, as a second layer of defense.*

Everly turned back to her bedroom door, turned the lock
to the unlocked position, and pulled on the knob. As the door
opened, she peeked her head outside to ensure nobody had
broken into her apartment. As expected, the place was dark and
empty.

Alright, she thought. *This is easily solved with a quick
experiment.*

With the door still open, Everly turned the lock, and
observed a metal bolt extend out from the door. She jiggled the
doorknob from the inside, and observed as the bolt didn't react.
She then jiggled the door from the outside, and observed that the
bolt was still unmoving. *Experiment successful,* she thought,
turning the lock to retract the bolt back to the unlocked position.

Everly shut the door, then turned the lock again. She
listened closely as the bolt extended into place. She then jiggled
the door, and confirmed it wouldn't open. *Alright. It's locked,
and from my experiment, I know it's still locked after I did that.*
She jiggled the door another time. Feeling satisfied it was indeed
still locked, she returned to her bed.

As Everly slid under the three layers of covers, she
gathered up her bedside dissertation, and placed it perfectly onto
the center of her nightstand.

"It's funny that I fell asleep without putting this away
first," she muttered under her breath.

Everly next picked up her crumpled blanket and
smoothed it out. As she wrapped the fluffy cloth around her
head, she let out a little whistle, followed by two teeth clicks and

a wink. *That's the last one for now*, she thought, wrapping the blanket taut over her mouth.

The fluffy sensation over her lips made her feel comfortable. Better yet, holding the blanket taut like this made it impossible for her to open her mouth (and thus, impossible for her to whistle). The fluffy cloth also seemed to block the space where that imaginary string needed to appear to pull on her eye. Everly signed through her nose at the feeling of relief, then closed her eyes and waited for sleep to reclaim her body.

2 | AWAKE

Everly awoke to the sound of soft music and birds chirping, both coming from a custom alarm on her phone. She opened her eyes with a yawn, slowly pushing a blanket off her face as she stretched her arms.

The young researcher gradually rolled out of bed, allowing the tension of her bed covers to caress her body in a slow, gentle descent to the floor. Everly let out a soft grumble as she crawled over to her shoes, removed her phone from the right shoe, and turned off the alarm.

Today's the day, she thought, lying on her back and staring up at the ceiling. She held her phone in front of her face, and opened her *To-Do List* app.

<u>Today</u>

7am – Calm Nerves w/Tea

9am – CBIT Appointment

11am – Lunch w/Family

12pm – Dissertation Defense: Setup

1:30pm – Dissertation Defense: Greet Committee

2pm – Dissertation Defense: Give Presentation

2:45pm – Dissertation Defense: Q&A

3:15pm – Cry and/or Celebrate

Oh. I should start brewing the tea, she thought. Everly climbed up the bedroom door, holding onto the doorknob to stabilize herself, then pushed herself up off the ground.

After picking her covers up off the floor and arranging them neatly over her bed, she unlocked her bedroom door, and meandered into the kitchen to start boiling some water.

Everly filled her tea kettle with filtered water, plugged it into the wall, and turned it on. Next, she opened a crickity wooden drawer attached to her countertop, from which she pulled out a small set of Bulgarian teas. These teas had been a birthday gift from her PhD advisor, Niko, many months ago. Everly picked out a green tea from the set, and plopped the small bag into her favorite mug.

As she waited for the water to boil, Everly returned to her bedroom to retrieve the printed copy of her dissertation from the nightstand where she'd left it. As she leafed through the pages, she unknowingly muttered her thoughts aloud, carefully practicing and perfecting each point she wanted to highlight during her defense this afternoon.

When the water was ready, she poured some into her mug. As the tea steeped, Everly delved back into perusing and rehearsing her research. Unconsciously, she chewed on the edges of her left hand while she read, leaving faint red marks along her fingers. After a few minutes, Everly put down her papers, and grabbed her readied drink. She then carefully brought the steaming drink out to her balcony, so she could enjoy it outside while watching the birds.

As she sat on a rickety wooden chair and blew a cooling breath into her tea, a fit of whistles, teeth clicks, and winks took effect. Everly let out a soft sign, and sipped her tea as best she could through the fit.

As she savored her drink, Everly reflected on the past six years she'd dedicated in pursuit of a singular goal: achieving her PhD. Along the way, she'd tasted great success, from securing a government internship with the Outer Space Exploration Agency, to embarking on a fruitful, multi-year co-op with a company called AccessibleML. In both instances, she'd thrived, infusing her own research ideas into her projects, and ultimately publishing papers before she left.

However, her journey hadn't been all roses and success stories. She also recalled numerous hours of mindlessly repetitive experiments, including a particularly grueling month where no progress seemed to be getting made.

Near the end of that month, she recalled a fight she'd had with Niko. The PhD advisor had said, "I think your idea will work, but we need to find the right <u>environment</u> in which it will work. Once we discover the best starting conditions, we can build on that to make your method more robust in general."

Everly had shouted at Niko after that remark, calling his strategy "a waste of time" and "basically probability hacking." She was wrong, of course. Niko simply knew far more about research than she did back then. Everly's response had stemmed from frustration with her initial exposure to the slow grind of research. Despite her outburst, Niko hadn't for a moment lost hope in the research idea she'd been exploring, and never deserved to be treated in such a way.

"FUCK!" burst from Everly's mouth, as the embarrassment of that memory crawled over her skin. "Fuck, fuck, fuck," she continued, wincing and involuntarily winking her left eye as these illicit tics escaped her mouth. Drips of scalding tea splashed into her lap in response to the abrupt jerking of her body.

Everly's eyes widened in alarm, as she immediately slapped a hand over her mouth, stifling any further sounds. Ignoring the burning sensation of hot tea on her legs, she looked around frantically, praying that none of her neighbors had noticed the outburst.

Thank goodness, nobody's walking their dog right now, she thought as she scanned the empty lawn below her balcony.

She took a few more glances at other nearby balconies. Once she was satisfied that no neighbors had witnessed her, she quickly finished her tea, then rushed back inside to clean herself off.

Everly returned to her bedroom, and after a quick shower in the connected bathroom, she donned the fancy outfit she'd set out for herself the night before.

Everly spent the next hour meticulously perfecting her appearance. She brushed her hair thoroughly, did her best to emphasize her freckles with some blush, tidied some stray eyebrow hairs, and wore a natural yet bold shade of lipstick.

After making some final touches, she stepped back and gazed at herself in the mirror. *Do I look like someone with a doctorate?* she mused. Everly turned about, flaunting her sharp and elegant attire. She draped her purse over her arm, and gave herself another thoughtful appraisal in the mirror. *I think so. Sure. Why not?* Satisfied, she gave one last twirl in the mirror, then made her way down to the parking lot just outside her apartment.

As she descended the musky, worn stairs of her apartment complex, a sudden thought halted her steps. *Did I lock the apartment on my way out?* she wondered. Everly turned on her heel, retraced her steps back up the stairs. Arriving at her apartment door, she gave the handle a firm jiggle. *Excellent,* she thought. She repeated the action. She then pulled the key out from her purse, slid it into the lock, slid it out, and jiggled the doorknob again. *Yep, that's locked,* she affirmed.

Don't want someone to break in and steal all my stuff while I'm gone, she mused, shoving the key back into her purse. *That would definitely put a damper on an already stressful day.* She jiggled the doorknob one more time, then resumed her descent down the stairs.

After she walked down just a couple steps, her ears perked up at the sound of a voice behind her.

"Didja say somethin'?" the voice asked. Everly turned, and recognized one of her neighbors now standing at the top of the staircase. He was a beefy man, wearing the same white t-shirt and jeans he always wore.

Everly's eyes flickered to the side before meeting the man's gaze. "No," she replied.

"I could'a sworn I heard, like, dissonant whispers, or something," the neighbor said, scratching his head as he spoke.

Ah, I must've been whispering my thoughts by accident when I was messing with the doorknob, Everly realized.

"Oh... maybe that *was* me, then," Everly admitted. "I have a big research presentation today."

"Huh," the man muttered.

"I was quietly rehearsing my research notes under my breath while I stepped out," Everly lied. It was often easier to fabricate explanations, than delve into her body's involuntarily behaviors. Whenever someone noticed a tic, a compulsive action, or her habit of thinking out loud, Everly generally opted to disclose as little as possible.

"Oh," the man responded.

Everly gave the man a blank stare for a few moments, expecting a customary "good luck with the presentation" or some similar sentiment. Instead, he returned her look with a blank stare of his own.

"Welp. Off I go, then," she said, returning to her descent down the staircase.

"You look good," the neighbor called after her. "You're real smart, too. I like that."

These words sent a chill down Everly's spine. On the surface, they were all compliments—kind words, which represented exactly how she wanted to appear to the world. However, something about the way this man spoke gave her a bad feeling in her gut—it was a feeling she couldn't quite explain, but she knew to trust her natural instincts in situations like this.

"Noted, but I'd prefer if you don't say those kinds of things to me again in the future, sir," she replied.

The man gave her a dismissive grunt in reply. Everly continued her descent, making her way to the parking lot.

As Everly sat down in her car, an uncomfortable pressure built up in her lungs. After plugging in her GPS and setting it to her occupational therapist's office for her 9am appointment, she let out a fit of expletive words, whistles, winks, clicks, squeaks, and head tilts. With each tic that came out of her, the mounting pressure weakened, becoming more bearable. Each tic that left felt like a burst of serotonin in her brain, getting rid of the bad feelings that built up during that uncomfortable interaction.

Everly's car, acting as a shield from the outside world, allowed her to unleash these tics without drawing unwelcome attention. For this, she felt grateful, as she turned the ignition and drove out of the parking lot.

3 | HELP

Everly let out a breath as she parked at the neurology clinic. *Don't worry about the dissertation for now,* she thought to herself. *For the next hour, this appointment is your top priority.*

Everly locked up her car, carefully jiggling the driver's and passenger's door handles to ensure the car was indeed locked, before heading into the clinic.

She entered the wide glass doors of the clean building, then sat down in a toy-filled waiting room. She checked into her appointment using an app on her phone, then absent-mindedly picked up a pamphlet sitting on a short wooden table in front of her.

"Help your child with CBIT: Comprehensive Behavioral Intervention for Tics," read the pamphlet's title. Everly flipped open the brochure, aiming to get her mind off the impending presentation that loomed over her afternoon.

The unfolded paper displayed numerous stock images of smiling children, with an advertisement for the neurology clinic proudly written in the center. Below that, was a short description: *"Comprehensive Behavioral Intervention for Tics (CBIT) is a structured therapeutic approach for reducing involuntary tics in individuals with Tourette Syndrome (TS), through the use of behavioral strategies."*

"Everly?" a voice asked from the secretarial counter. Everly looked up from her reading, observing as a small boy emerged from the OT's office, holding hands with his mother. "We're ready for you," the receptionist continued.

Everly nodded, placing the pamphlet back down on the table in front of her. She stood, covered to her mouth to stifle a yawn, then made her way into the office of Dr. Rachel Nest.

"Hello," Everly uttered, stepping into the office. Dr. Nest looked elegant as usual, pulling out some papers for this appointment. Although the woman didn't look frazzled at all, Everly liked to imagine her presence was a welcome break from the OT's usual pediatric patients.

"Good morning," the occupational therapist replied, offering Everly a seat. "You're looking sharp! What's the occasion?"

"I have my defense today," Everly responded, sitting down. "I've been preparing for it all week, so here's an apology in advance if I'm a little frazzled this morning."

"Oh, that's today!" Dr. Nest exclaimed. "Did you want to reschedule this appointment, so you can focus on preparing?"

"No, no," Everly said. "I consider this part of my preparations. I want a strategy for the whistling tic today, because it's been flaring up and I don't want it interfering with my presentation."

"Certainly, we can do that," the therapist agreed, clicking her pen to make a note on some paper as she spoke. "In that case, let's start off by discussing last week's progress with the coprolalia."

"That's...the swearing tics, right?" Everly asked, some blood rushing to her face.

Dr. Nest nodded. "Remember, there's no need to be embarrassed, Everly. I meet with patients that have these kinds of tics all day."

"Okay...," Everly said, thinking back to how her week went. "Well, most days, I practiced the competing response for half an hour, like I'm supposed to. I might've missed a few days since I've been crazy busy."

"Last week, you told me you felt 'a build-up of pressure in your lungs and throat, eventually resulting in sort of an explosion from your mouth to let the tic out.' As a competing response, we decided on tightening your diaphragm, since that makes it difficult to use your vocal cords in such a way. Do you still feel that's a good competing response for this?" the therapist queried.

"Yea, it definitely helps block those tics," Everly affirmed. "There were a couple times in the research lab that I normally would've excused myself outside to swear, but instead, I was able to do the diaphragm thing to stay at my computer and keep working."

"Very good," the therapist muttered, writing down some more notes.

"Although, this morning, I was outside on my balcony and a few of the... um, fucks, flew out from my mouth before I could notice," Everly continued. "I was super distracted at the time, thinking about my defense today, so that's probably why—but I totally forgot to do the competing response. I think I might've let some swears out in the car, on my way here, too."

"Well, this week, your task was just to practice the competing response for 30 minutes each day," Dr. Nest replied. "Although now that we're through with the week, I'd like you to keep doing that response whenever you sense that build-up of pressure again, alright?"

Everly nodded.

"If you find that you're struggling to notice the build-up in time to do the competing response for these tics, let me know, and we'll discuss some more strategies," Dr. Nest continued.

"Okay," Everly agreed.

"Great," the therapist said, putting her hands together. "Then, let's move on to discussing that whistling tic. Do you think you'll be able to reproduce it for me?"

"Yea... it's been happening a lot," Everly replied. She gave a nervous laugh, "...although I really hate this part."

"I understand, but remember, you don't need to suppress in front of me," the woman assured. "I know you tend to bundle up your tics in front of people, until they come out when you're alone, but this is a safe space."

Everly nodded, letting out a deep sigh as she did.

"Let's talk for five minutes," Dr. Nest continued, noting the time from a small clock on her desk. "We'll talk about anything you want. Don't suppress any tics while we're talking. When you notice the whistle tic happened, raise your index finger like this." The therapist pointed towards upwards with her left hand.

Everly nodded. She'd done this same process for different tics during past appointments, so she knew what to expect.

"Let's get started," the woman continued. "Do you want to... tell me about your map collection?"

Everly's eyes lit up with excitement, and she felt her guard lower. Immediately, the tug of an imaginary string appeared on her right eyelid. The string pulled down, forcing her to tilt her head slightly to the right. As she winked her right eye, she let out a whistle, followed by two teeth clicks and another wink. In response, the pull of the string loosened, as if rewarding her for giving into the whistle.

"Yes," Everly replied, pointing her right finger towards the ceiling as she spoke. "I'd love to talk about that."

The therapist looked at Everly's finger, then looked down, writing something in her notebook. "Tell me about your favorite," she asked as she wrote.

"Oh, man, I don't think I can pick one," Everly said, looking up at the ceiling. Another whistle tic came on, and she didn't resist it. "Oop, that's another," Everly noted, pointing her index finger towards the sky.

"Very good," Dr. Nest assured.

"I guess…" Everly pondered, continuing to signal the therapist with each tic she noticed while speaking. "…I'll give you two answers. My first answer is from a vintage book I found at a pawn shop. The book is called *The Eras Atlas of the Earth*, and among other things, it has this map of ancient Europe, Africa, and Asia. It's really neat, because there's elaborate drawings of sea monsters out in the uncharted waters, including where America's supposed to be!" Everly chuckled, then sighed, frustrated by the imaginary tugging string that seemed to gain a strong hold over her eye.

"You said you had two answers?" the therapist prodded. Everly whistled, clicked her teeth twice, and winked—then pointed her index finger to the sky. "Very good," Dr. Nest continued, scribbling away in her book.

"*bitch*—sorry!" Everly said, slapping a hand over her mouth.

"It's okay, Everly," Dr. Nest reassured, "just focus on pointing out your whistles, and don't worry about any other tics, alright?"

Everly nodded, but tightened her diaphragm to block future outbursts. The action didn't seem to have any impact on her whistles or the imaginary string pulling her eye, but it did put some of the mounting pressure she felt into disarray, effectively blocking the conditions needed for her to involuntarily swear again.

"My second answer…" Everly continued, adjusting her breathing and voice to flow smoothly while her diaphragm was tightened, "…is an old campus map from my university's archives. My advisor, Niko, gave it to me as a gift many years ago. I still don't know how he managed to get something like that permanently out of the archives for me, but it's an authentic map they displayed in the student union right after it was built. From it, you can see that the school started with just some basic classrooms for mathematics and other liberal arts stuff, one dorm building, the union itself, and a single football field. There weren't even any computers on campus back then—let alone the technology center we have today!"

Everly's eyes glowed with glee as she continued to describe the intricate details she'd noticed on her two favorite maps. While she spoke, she diligently acknowledged her tics for the therapist. Eventually, Dr. Nest glanced at the clock and put down her pen.

"Looks like we've hit five minutes," she observed. "I noticed your whistling tic 17 times, and you noticed it all of those times as well."

Everly gave a light smile. She knew this wasn't a test, but if it had been, it felt as if she'd gotten a perfect score.

"I've also noticed that it's not *just* the whistle," the therapist continued. "Your whistle is always accompanied by a complex series of tics, with a consistent order: a rightwards head tilt, then a right eye wink, the whistle, some teeth mashing to make a sound, and finally another right eye wink. Have you noticed these other tics, too?"

"I think… the head tilt, and the right eye wink always go together," Everly replied. "Separately, the whistle is always followed by the teeth clicks and the eye wink. However, I think of that as two separate series, not one series of five."

"Interesting," the therapist stated, picking up her pen and writing some more notes. "During our conversation, those two series always happened together: the head tilt with the wink first, then the whistle with everything that comes after it. Have you noticed in your daily life that those two series of tics tend to have some correlation?"

"I think the two series of tics definitely happen on their own sometimes," Everly countered. "However, when they do happen together... I guess, yea, the head tilt one usually starts off the whole series."

"For today, would you like us to just focus on the three tics that happen with the whistling, or all five tics that start from the head tilt?" Dr. Nest asked.

"Well, I don't want *any* of them to happen during my presentation later today," Everly worried. "Could... could we do both?"

"Yes, let's do them both simultaneously for this week's session, and see how it goes," the therapist agreed. "Just to clarify—it sounds like the head tilt leads to the wink, which *sometimes* leads to the whistle, and then the whistle leads to the teeth clicks and the second wink. Does that sound correct?"

Everly thought for a moment, then nodded in agreement.

"In that case, let's focus on two tics: the head tilt, and the whistle," Dr. Nest stated. "If you can detect and prevent just those, then I think the whole series of tics will fall apart, since those other tics only ever happen *after* a head tilt or whistle."

"Okay," Everly agreed. "That makes sense to me."

"It seems you're aware when these tics are happening," Dr. Nest continued. "At least, you're aware of the whistle since we focused on that one during our conversation and you acknowledged them all. For the next step: do you feel any sort of urge or inkling *before* either of these tics happen?"

"Yes," Everly replied. "For the head tilt, I definitely feel an urge. It feels like an invisible string is attached to my right eyelid, and it's being pulled on, maybe by like a hand that's grabbing it, or a tiny anvil that's tied to the end of it, or something."

Dr. Nest flipped her notebook open to another page, and started scribbling notes while Everly spoke. "That means I must tilt my head and wink my eye," Everly continued. "It's sort of like I'm being physically forced to do it."

"Do you still feel this string, right now?" Dr. Nest questioned. Everly nodded.

"Do you feel the pull?" Dr. Nest asked. Everly nodded again, then tilted her head, winked, whistled, clicked her teeth, and winked again.

"Does the feeling change if you resist tilting your head and winking?" Dr. Nest prodded.

"Yes!" Everly exclaimed. "It gets stronger and stronger, until I can't resist it anymore."

"If you *could* resist it more, do you think something bad would eventually happen?" the therapist questioned.

"Absolutely," Everly replied. "That's exactly what I feel like. I'm worried the string will rip my eyelid off, or maybe just tug so hard that, when my head tilts, it snaps my neck and I die."

Everly put a hand over her neck protectively, displeased by the thought. "I mean... I know that *wouldn't* happen, since the string is completely imaginary," she clarified. "It just *feels* like that, sometimes, yaknow?"

"Sure," Dr. Nest replied, nodding as she scribbled away in her notebook. "Do you feel anything else before the head tilt?"

Everly thought for a moment, scratching her nose as she did. "No," she replied.

"How about for the whistle? You said this series of tics sometimes starts at the whistle step, correct?" Dr. Nest questioned. The therapist moved her hands as she spoke, as if gesturing to some step in a timeline of tics that she'd visualized in her mind. "Do you notice any urges or precursors in the instances where the whistle happens, separate from the rightwards head tilt?"

"Hmmm…" Everly pondered. "Well, now that you mentioned the thing about the series of five tics, the eye wink or head tilt is probably *one* precursor," she admitted. "However, in the cases where it isn't… hmmm…"

Everly straightened her head, and tried to ignore the feeling of the string for a moment. She let some air into her lungs, and shaped her mouth into an O, as if daring the whistling tic to start.

After a moment, she felt a light pressure in her chest and head. Her neck tilted forwards, and she let out a soft whistle, then immediately clicked her teeth twice and winked her right eye. Dr. Nest observed Everly with interest as she did this.

"I felt a pressure in my chest. Much lighter than the pressure I feel before the swearing tics," Everly stated. The therapist immediately started writing notes. "I also kind of… get, like, a headache," Everly continued. "After that, it feels like a tiny gust of wind needs to get out of my throat, so I sort of naturally turn my mouth into an O shape and position my head to let it flow out."

"Yes, I noticed you tilted your head *forwards* that time," Dr. Nest said. "Do you always tilt your head forwards before whistling, if you're not already tilting it to the right side due to the other tic?"

"I guess, maybe? I've never noticed that before," Everly replied with a shrug.

"Alright, let's do another conversation," Dr. Nest said, glancing at her clock. "This time, do your signal when you feel the *urge* for either of these tics," she explained. "Point *one* finger towards the sky if you're about to tilt your head and do the whole series with all the tics, and point *two* fingers if you're about to just whistle and do the smaller set of tics. Does that make sense?"

"Yes," Everly agreed.

"Great," Dr. Nest said, clicking her pen and tapping it to a fresh page in her notebook. "Tell me about your 3rd favorite map from your collection."

"Oh, I don't know if I can give you one answer to that," Everly chuckled. "Can I give two answers again?"

"Of course," the therapist replied.

Everly felt a tug on her eyelid. She then tilted her head, winked her eye, whistled, clicked her teeth, and winked again. "Wait, I saw that one coming," Everly claimed, pointing one finger to the sky. "I forgot to point up my finger, but I felt the urge."

"Very good," Dr. Nest said.

"Are you counting that one as an urge that I caught, or an urge that I missed?" Everly asked.

"Just keep telling me about your map, and do your best to point out the urges as you feel them," the woman replied.

"Right, the map. I have two answers," Everly continued. "The first one is a language distribution map across the planet, which is color-coded by different dialects as well. The reason I love it so much, though, is the story of how I got it."

"Mmm hmm," Dr. Nest hummed attentively. Everly pointed two fingers towards the ceiling, before letting out a whistle and the other tics that went with it.

"So, this was back when I was a freshman getting my undergraduate degree," Everly cheered. "One day, I was at the university's bookstore, and I found that beautiful map inside a linguistics textbook. I asked if I could make a quick color copy it on a printer, and they said I couldn't unless I bought the whole textbook. Then, they said the book was in limited quantity, so only people taking this one specific linguistics class could buy it. Worse, that specific linguistics class was only available to students majoring in linguistics."

As Everly spoke, she continued to signal the precursory feelings of tugging string and light pressure to her therapist. "Now, I hadn't picked out my major yet, but I *was* in the honors program. That meant I could pick any major I wanted from of any school at the university, and my application would be instantly approved."

Everly chuckled, pleased with where this story was going. "So, I used that immediately become a linguistic major. Then, I signed up for that specific class that only linguistics majors could sign up for. After that, I purchased the textbook with my mom's credit card, made a beautiful copy of the map I wanted with the library copy machine, and then immediately returned the textbook."

Everly let out some involuntary squeaks and swears, as she took a moment to laugh at her own story. "Next, I immediately unregistered from the linguistics class, and took some other classes I needed to take instead. I was technically a linguistics major for the rest of the semester, but then I switched to my double degree in computer science and mathematics, and I stuck with that for the rest of my time there."

"Let's cut off our conversation there," Dr. Nest announced. "How did that feel? I noticed you did the whistling series twice, and the full series 11 times. You seemed generally quite aware when the urges were coming, so I think a competing response should do well for you in these cases."

"Okay," Everly nodded. She felt disappointed that she hadn't gotten to explain her second answer to the 'third favorite map' question yet, but also, she knew from prior experience that Dr. Nest was likely going to ask for one more conversation before the appointment was over.

"I've got some ideas for your competing responses, here," the therapist said. "First, for the rightwards head tilt. I would like you to tilt you head ever-so-slightly to the *left* as soon as you feel that string on your right eyelid. Instead of looking like a tic, it'll look like you're just tilting your head slightly to express interest in your conversation with someone. Meanwhile, the slight leftwards head tilt should contract your neck's muscles in a way completely inverse to how they'd need to contract for your tic. This should effectively block the tic."

Everly tilted her head slightly to the left. She felt the string tugging on her right eyelid, and squeezed it closed in response—but her head did not feel the need to tilt rightwards anymore. "Alright," Everly agreed. "What about my right eyelid, though? I still feel like it's going to get ripped off by the string."

"Try blinking your eyes in union, at a slow pace with a consistent rhythm," the therapist suggested. "That should help you take control of those muscles, so your right eye can't wink involuntarily."

Everly obliged, slow blinking rhythmically while tilting her head slightly to the left. The string powerlessly pulled on her eyelid, unable to make anything budge.

"This is why I like CBIT," Everly cheered. "I feel like I'm taking control of my body again, because I'm just doing something else that I can control, rather than trying to resist the tics."

"That's the goal!" Dr. Nest happily agreed. "Now, for the whistling. Press the tip of your tongue against the roof of your mouth, and hold it there."

Everly did as instructed. "Now, try to whistle," Dr. Nest commanded.

At the sound of the word 'whistle,' Everly's body immediately tried to whistle tic. Her neck pushed forwards slightly, and a light gust of wind escaped her mouth—silently, as her raised tongue entirely disrupted the airflow needed to produce a whistling sound.

Without the whistling sound, Everly felt no compulsion to click her teeth or wink her eye. "Very good!" Dr. Nest cheered. How did that feel?"

"I think I still moved my neck forwards, but that certainly stopped the whistle," Everly replied.

"For the neck pulling forwards, also try just tilting your head slightly to the left," Dr. Nest suggested. "That should lock up your neck muscles from doing the tic, just like with tilting to the right."

"Okay," Everly nodded.

"I think... because we're kind of doing two tics this session, we're starting to run out of time," Dr. Nest observed. "We don't have a full 5 minutes left. Let's just do a 3-minute conversation, and see how these competing responses are working, alright?"

"Sure," Everly agreed.

"During this conversation, whenever you feel *either* of the urges coming on, I want to you tilt your head slightly to the left, and blink your eyes in a consistent rhythm—since a head tilting and a winking element exists in both series of tics," Dr. Nest explained. "Furthermore, if you feel the pressure from the whistle coming on, I want to you tap your tongue to the roof of your mouth, in addition to tilting your head and blinking your eyes. Got it?"

"Yes," Everly said, eager to finish her map story.

"As usual, when you feel a tic coming, do your competing response for whichever is longer: one minute, or until the urge goes away," Dr. Nest clarified. "If this means you need to stare at me in silence for the full three minutes, that's perfectly fine."

"I'm ready," Everly agreed. The therapist gestured for Everly to continue. "Alright," Everly cheered. She tilted her head to the left, started blinking her eyes in a consistent pattern, and tapped her tongue to the roof of her mouth.

Quickly realizing that she couldn't talk while holding her tongue to the roof of her mouth, Everly decided to stop doing that one until she felt the need to whistle. The head tilt and blinking, however, she continued to do, constantly thwarting the imaginary string's pull on her eyelid.

"So, I have another answer to your question about my third favorite map," Everly said. "I have an OSEA star map from an old astronomy magazine. Back when I did an internship with OSEA, I had shown pictures of my map collection to my internship mentor. After we published a paper together from my work over that summer, and she gave it to me as a celebratory gift!"

Everly felt a whistle coming on, and blocked it by pushing the tip of her tongue to the roof of her mouth. She glanced at the therapist's clock, and waited a full minute, while the light pressure in her head and throat slowly dispelled.

"Very good," Dr. Nest praised, writing some notes down while the two sat in silence.

After a minute, Everly dropped her tongue again, and finished her story. "Um, yea. Where was I? So, my OSEA mentor actually gave me the magazine in-person when we met up at the research conference where our work was published! It was really sweet, and great to see her in-person again, since our publication happened about a year after my internship had officially ended."

"That sounds wonderful," Dr. Nest agreed. "Unfortunately, it looks like we're at our time, and I have another patient to get to. How did the competing responses work for you? From my end, it looked like they were working quite well!"

"Yes, they definitely were!" Everly cheered.

"That's great to hear," the woman replied. "As usual, I'd like for you to repeat this exercise for 30 minutes every day for the rest of the week. Just sit down, and do these three responses whenever you feel the urge for their respective tics. Additionally, try to start integrating the diaphragm tightening into your daily life, whenever you feel the coprolalia urge coming on. Sound good?" Everly gave the therapist two thumbs-up in reply.

"If you have any other questions or concerns we didn't get to today, you can feel free to reach out to my office with a message," Dr. Nest continued. "Otherwise, I'll see you next week—and best of luck with your dissertation defense! You're a delightfully smart person, so I'm confident you'll do well!" Dr. Nest gave Everly a cheerful smile.

Everly felt warm inside. The occupational therapist's compliment felt like it was coming from a place of sincerity. "Thank you," Everly said, returning the smile.

As Everly emerged from the occupational therapist's doorway, she was quickly replaced by pair of parents entering the office with their child. Everly tilted her head slightly to the left, and starting blinking intentionally.

"See you next time!" Everly said to the receptionist, as she walked through the waiting area.

Upon stepping outside, Everly looked at her car with a foreboding terror.

Something like 4 hours until my dissertation defense starts, she mused. *I remember when it was 6 YEARS until my dissertation defense starts. How did time move so quickly?*

With a nervous gulp, Everly sat down in her car, stuck her key in the ignition, and drove off to campus.

4 | FAMILY

Everly's car chugged through the light snowfall, inching to a stop just outside the student union. The young researcher parked in a prime spot—likely, only available because most undergraduates had left early for winter break.

After locking her car doors two times each, Everly put her hood up, her hands in her pockets, and trudged into the nearby brick building.

"There she is," Everly's father cheered with a warm smile. Her parents had been standing just inside the union, likely watching as Everly's car had pulled into the lot.

"It's so good to see you," her mother exclaimed, pulling Everly into a stiff hug.

Everly tilted her head slightly to the left, tightened her diaphragm, tapped her tongue to the roof of her mouth, and began blinking in a slow, controlled fashion. "It's good to see you guys, too," she muttered, her voice slightly muffled by her competing responses. Everly felt a strong tension under her right eyelid, and an explosive pressure building in her chest. Yet, she couldn't bear the embarrassment of releasing a tic in such a public space—let alone, in front of her parents.

"Are you okay, honey? You sound quiet," her mother observed. The middle-aged woman held Everly by both of her shoulders, and looked into the young researcher's eyes.

"It's just nerves," Everly lied, splitting her attention between her parents and fighting her tics. "Today's a big day for me, after all."

"Everly. You'll do great," her father comforted. He didn't touch Everly, but his eyes gleamed lovingly, reminiscent of the morning sun.

"Let's get something to eat!" Everly announced, changing the subject. "Assuming I do finish my PhD today, I need to have a terrible chicken sandwich from this place one last time."

Everly led her parents down the white-tiled floors of the student union, and into a moderately-clean dining center. While her folks split off to get sushi and salad, Everly walked up to the grungy grilling station. She glanced at a sweaty man flipping burgers, then scanned her student card and swiped a chicken sandwich off the shelf.

Everly took a deep breath as she brought her crispy meal over to an indoor picnic table. An old, but all-to-familiar pressure started mounting at the top of her head—begging her to tap the tips of both her ears simultaneously. *That's a surprise. This is an old tic,* she mused. Everly set her meal down on the table, then sat and placed her hands flat over her thighs. *I must be pretty nervous,* she pondered. *I haven't had to fight this tic for months. My nerves must be letting it resurface.* As the mounting pressure in her head begged for the relief of a quick ear tap, Everly held strong, keeping her hands flat and away from her ears.

"So, what's the plan for today?" Everly's mother asked, joining her at the table with a plate full of raw fish. "You're going straight to the research center after this, right? Do you want a ride?"

Everly nodded. "It's not too far to walk, but it would be great to stay out of the cold. So, I will take that ride. Thank you," she cheered.

The young researcher then placed a hand over her mouth. *Fuck, Fuck, Fuck!* she mouthed, lowing her voice to the softest possible whisper. She then quickly picked up her sandwich, and took a bite. Her mother seemed oblivious to the action—she likely assumed Everly had just covered her mouth to yawn, or to chew.

Everly reveled as an addictive sense of relief flowed through her body. The silent swearing didn't feel as good as screaming slurs in the privacy of her own home, but it did greatly relieve the sense of pressure in her chest as it overflowed her body with happy-feeling chemicals. Even the ear-tapping pressure in her head rewarded her, by subsiding in response to the successful tic.

The competing responses are helpful, Everly thought as she loosened her diaphragm, *but sometimes, letting some tics out is just so much easier.*

As Everly's father sat down with his bowl of salad, the young researcher offered him a potato wedge from her chicken meal. "No, but thank you," he replied, waving off the fry.

Everly stared at him blankly, still offering the wedge as she silently counted in her head. After about 4 seconds of mixing his plate of salad, the brown-haired man caved, accepting the fry from his daughter and tossing it down his gullet.

"I hope my presentation will go well," Everly said, returning to take another bite from her sandwich.

"You've been preparing for so long, honey," Everly's mother replied. Her father grunted in agreement, as he shoveled a scoop of arugula into his mouth.

"I know; my presentation's perfect," Everly concurred. "I've practiced it more times than I can count, and my publications tell a cohesive story."

Everly's father gave her a thumbs-up while shoving another scoop of salad down the hatch. Everly's mother stabbed a piece of sashimi with a chopstick, as if she were spear-fishing, then pulled it off the utensil with her teeth.

"However," Everly muttered, looking down at her meal, "I'm worried about keeping my cool up there."

"You said it yourself, Evie," her mom replied. "You've practiced this presentation more times than you can count!" The woman made a supportive fist in the air as she spoke.

"No, but I'm worried about the *other* thing," Everly countered, lowering her voice. Her parents gave her a quizzical look. "The tics," Everly clarified, lowering her voice even more. "They've been really bad this week, and have gotten even worse today."

"Look, Everly, for what it's worth—we haven't noticed a single tic today," her mom replied. "Honestly, half the time, we forget you even have Tourette's, honey." With his mouth full, Everly's dad nodded in agreement.

Lower your voice, woman! Everly thought to herself. "That's… kind of the point," the young scholar replied, "since I'm always fighting the tics. My worry is, what if I mess up because I'm splitting my focus between the tics and the presentation?"

"Well, why don't you do that CBIT stuff?" her mother pitched. "That helps you, right?"

"Yes, mom, that is what I'll be doing," Everly replied. "I even had another CBIT session this morning. It still might not be enough, though."

"If you can't block a tic, just play it off and keep going," her dad piped up. "They'll forget what they saw, and focus on your presentation."

"What if they discriminate against me, because they notice and realize I'm not normal?" Everly worried. "I want to use this PhD to become a professor. What if they think I wouldn't be good at teaching, because I'm disabled?"

41

"Everyone's got something," her father said. "Don't fret about it."

"Yes, don't worry about it," her mother agreed. "You are going to do great! Not to mention, again, that I have not noticed a single tic from you today!"

"Alright. Thanks, you two," Everly sighed. She tilted her a little bit to the left, and blinked her eyes rhythmically as she took another bite from her sandwich. *You haven't noticed them, because I've been working my ass off to hide them this whole time,* she pondered. *I guess that's hard to understand.*

"How's the sandwich?" her dad questioned.

Everly shrugged. "I've had better, but it's not raw. One time, this place gave me chicken sandwich that was completely raw. It was gross."

Her dad broke into a laughing fit, which shifted into a coughing fit after a few seconds. "You have some low standards, Everly," he chuckled, gathering himself. "You want your chicken not raw. That seems pretty reasonable to me!"

Everly smiled. With the subject of conversation changed, the grip of her tics over her mind slightly weakened. "You think that's bad? One time my friend found a literal razor blade in her food from the Indian station!" Everly exclaimed.

"No way!" Everly's mother gasped.

"A manager said it must've fallen off the machine that prepares the food before sending it here," Everly continued. "Plus, because we showed it to the manager, my friend got the meal comped! I think I've got a picture of the razor blade on my phone; let me show you!"

Everly spent the rest of the lunch laughing with her parents about various little stories from her time at this university—a momentarily relief from the career-defining presentation that loomed ever closer.

After their lunch came to an end, Everly joined her parents in a dusty minivan they'd had since she was a child. As the vehicle's more-than-a-decade-old engine choked to life, sweat formed over Everly's brow, and the mounting pressure of her tics started to return.

Everly practiced her competing responses in the back seat, not saying much while her parents navigated to the research center.

"Come back at one-thirty, okay? My defense starts a two o'clock," Everly announced as they arrived to the center. The young scholar hopped out from the car, and onto the sidewalk just outside the main entrance. "In the meantime, I'll be setting up with Niko, 'kay?"

"Understood, honey. Good luck! We'll come back at one-thirty to support you!" her mother reiterated.

"Yes, good luck!" her father added.

As her parents drove off somewhere to pass the time for the next hour and a half, Everly gave the minivan a grim look.

"The next time I sit in that car, I'll be either an academic with a PhD, or a failure with hopeless dreams," she muttered.

.

5 | NERVES

"That seems way overdramatic," a voice countered from behind Everly.

"Uah!" the scholar jumped, turning around and holding out her hands defensively.

"The council has already reviewed your dissertation," the voice continued. Niko's familiar face popped up from behind a pile of snow lining the research building. "If we don't like what you have to say, it's more probable that we'd approve your PhD on the condition you complete some final revisions, than outright fail you. It's extremely rare to leave a defense with no path forward. I wouldn't have let you defend if I thought that was a possibility."

"What—Wait, What—Niko? Why are you here?" Everly stuttered.

"I'm supposed to help you set up, and I'm also part of the council," Niko replied. "Why wouldn't I be here?"

"No," Everly laughed. "Why are you outside, and creeping around in the snow?"

"I'm not creeping around," Niko replied defensively, standing up and brushing his curly hair with his fingers. The man's prickly face implied he'd forgotten to shave this morning, but besides that, his sharp suit and bright bowtie gave off an aura of elegance.

"I forgot my keycard to get into the center," Niko explained. "It's just an RFID card, so a long time ago, I made a copy and hid it in a fake rock under the bushes. Although, it's hard to find with all the snow around."

"I can just let you in," Everly chuckled, showing her student card.

"Well, *now* you can," Niko agreed, stepping onto the sidewalk and flicking some snow off his pants. "I wasn't just going to wait for you when I had a spare lying around somewhere, though."

"Did you find it?" Everly questioned.

"No, it's still somewhere under all the snow," Niko answered.

"Alright, then just follow me inside," Everly offered.

The two walked around to the front of the building, and Everly swiped her card against a scanner to unlock it. As she pulled open the heavy glass doors, a wide marble staircase donned with portraits of past alumni welcomed her.

"Isn't it a security risk to leave copies of your ID around?" Everly asked.

"It's hidden in a fake rock, which is slightly buried under a bush," Niko replied. "Even if someone somehow managed to stumble across it, they wouldn't know what they found. It just looks like a blank RFID card, but with my credentials loaded into it."

Everly tsked as the two walked up the marble staircase to the second floor, then pushed open the second conference room door on the left. *That is classic Niko,* she thought, feeling amused. *His first ever student's about to defend, yet he's acting no different than he would any other day.*

As Niko rushed into the room to start booting up the central computer, Everly felt the familiar and unwelcome sensation of a string tugging down on her right eyelid. Before the tension could pull her head to the right, Everly tilted her head to the left. Before the string could force her right eye to wink, Everly began blinking in a rhythmic fashion—retaking that control.

"Niko," Everly stated suddenly. The young researcher scanned the room with paranoia, ensuring the two of them were absolutely alone before she continued. "Remember those tics I've told you about? They've been rather heavy today. I'm worried about them messing up my PhD defense. Thoughts?"

Niko looked at Everly as he stepped up onto the conference table, then looked up as he poked the power button on a brick-shaped projector attached to the ceiling. "Everly. If you tic, that's okay."

Everly took a step back with surprise from that answer. "I plan to conceal them as best I can," she countered.

"You don't have to," Niko replied. The tall research advisor hopped off the conference table, then flicked off some dirt he'd left on it from his shoes. "My earlier offer still stands, though. I'm happy to tell the other council members about your concern, so they know what's up before you defend."

"No, I'd rather keep my condition hidden," Everly replied. "If someone *were* to tell them, I'd want it to be me."

"Sure," Niko agreed with a shrug. He then glanced at Everly, holding eye contact for a moment. "Again, though, if you don't conceal and you let out tics… that's fine."

Everly stared back at him, stunned by his response. "…thanks," she said after a few moments. "In my heart, I guess I always knew that… *should* be the way to approach these things. Nobody's ever said it to me, before, though."

"Happy to help," Niko replied matter-of-factly. He then turned back to the computer, navigated to the login screen, and looked up to verify the screen was successfully being projected onto the wall of the conference room.

"We've got, like, over an hour before the remainder of the council arrives. Do you want to log in, and run through the presentation a few times?" Niko pitched.

"Absolutely," Everly agreed, hanging her coat and heading over to the computer.

The young researcher took a deep breath as she clicked open her document, and watched the projector paint her title slide upon the far wall of the conference room. The tugging string on Everly's right eye seemed to momentarily glitch and freeze as her body flooded with adrenaline.

The final copy of my presentation is really up there, Everly mused. *I've been in this conference room hundreds of times, but today feels different. I'm going to shine today...*

A burst of pressure suddenly appeared in Everly's lungs, forcing its way up through her mouth in an attempt to whistle. The young researcher immediately snapped the tip of her tongue to the roof of her mouth—disrupting the forceful flow of air, and subduing the whistling tic completely.

...and I'm not going to drop my guard, either, she fumed.

6 | CONCEAL

For the next hour or so, Everly practiced her defense with Niko in the conference room.

As 1:30pm started to roll around, Everly set her presentation back to the title slide, and prepared to greet her audience at the door.

"This is good," Niko said, swinging one of the room's double doors open, while Everly pulled open the other. "Not a single last-minute change was needed. Your presentation is very organized, and you tell a cohesive story. I think this will go well."

"I hope so," Everly agreed, gritting her teeth as she blocked the room open with a pair of door stoppers.

"Alright. You stay here, and greet everyone as they come in—particularly the council members," Niko ordered. "I'll run down front, open the door to let people into the building, and direct them up the stairs."

"Sounds good," Everly agreed.

The research advisor snapped his fingers into two finger guns, then trotted to the bottom of the marble staircase, leaving Everly alone outside the conference room.

The young researcher took in a big breath, then let it out as a sigh which turned into a nervous yawn. She felt a light pressure over her head again—the feeling of that old tic, begging her to tap the tips of her ears with her index fingers.

Even though nobody's around, I'm going to resist all tics right now, Everly concluded. While she made this determination in her mind, her hands absent-mindedly lifted up and tapped the tips of her ears.

Oops, Everly thought, bringing her hands down to her waist and interlacing her fingers. *Starting now, I'm going to resist all tics.*

Like clockwork, her body responded to the challenge by sensing a buildup of air in her lungs. Everly felt an overwhelming desire to whistle come over her—an action which would surely lead to subsequent teeth clicks and a wink. Defiant, Everly tapped the tip of her tongue to the roof of her mouth, began blinking rhythmically, and tilted her head slightly to the left for good measure.

"Am I first?" a voice asked from the top of the marble staircase. Everly glanced over a fit, black-haired woman donned with a purse and snappy dress. It was Chelsea—one of Everly's closest friends.

"Yea. You were supposed to wait, so the council members could get here first," Everly teased.

"I was?" the woman questioned, her face turning red.

"No," Everly chuckled. "I'm just kidding. You're perfectly fine, Chelsea. Thanks for coming!"

Chelsea mimed wiping sweat off her brow, then strut towards the conference room. "Good. Just wanted to support you, Evie! Good luck! You're so smart; you're going to do great!"

"Thanks, Chels," Everly replied, pulling her friend in for a hug. "You can sit anywhere in the conference room. Just leave the front few seats open for the council."

"Oh yea, I'll be totally out-of-the-way," Chelsea agreed as she stepped into the room. She then turned back to face Everly, and her face sparked upon seeing the top of the stairs. "Oop, I see more people coming. I'll shut up now—you go greet them. Good luck, girl!"

"Thank you," Everly repeated, turning to greet the new guests while Chelsea took a seat.

The next group was a huddle of three men. Everly recognized them immediately, as younger students from Niko's research lab. Of course, they were here to support Niko's oldest student, but more so they probably wanted a first-hand experience at what defending might look like for them in the future.

"Kai, Daniel, Matt. Thanks for coming," Everly greeted the trio. The young scholar kept strong on her tic-countering techniques as she spoke. She didn't know these three very well, so she'd feel more embarrassed if they were to learn of her condition.

Immediately behind the boys trotted Finlay Peart. He was an elderly gentleman with wrinkly skin and not a hair left on his head. He walked slowly, with the support of a simple wooden cane. Everly recognized him as one of the three council members set to judge her defense today, along with Niko and one other professor.

"It's an honor to have you here, Dr. Peart," Everly greeted. As the three boys from Niko's lab made their way to their seats, Everly offered a handshake to the elderly council member.

"Ah, I'm nuthin' special," Dr. Peart replied, accepting Everly's handshake with a light touch. "I'm just an old man that likes to learn."

"You published nearly a hundred foundational machine learning papers in the '60s and '70s," Everly countered. "You laid a lot of the groundwork for what I'm presenting today. It's really an honor to have you here."

"Oh, posh," Dr. Peart waved off the compliment. "Decided to butter me up before I see your defense today, eh?" he joked.

"Maybe a little," Everly joked back with a polite laugh. "Would you like any help finding your seat?"

"Naw, I'm good," Dr. Peart replied. "I've walked into this conference room more times than I've walked into my own home."

"Heh, alright," Everly chuckled. "Well, thank you for coming, and I look forwards to sharing my work with you."

"I look forwards to learning something new from you," the man replied, waving Everly off as he trod into the conference space.

Everly faced the stairs again, where she saw her parents awkwardly moving out-of-the-way to allow a slender council member, Sofia Caruso, to get to Everly first.

Everly felt her heart skip a beat with each *CLACK!* the woman's pristine high-heeled shoes made against the tiled floors of the research center. The tall professor walked with confidence and purpose. Dr. Caruso was famous for her keen awareness to cut off research projects that weren't going anywhere, even during the earliest stages of their development.

"Everly Hawthorne," the woman acknowledged, offering a hand.

The young scholar took the council member's hand in her own, shaking it with a firm grip as she looked up into the professor's stern blue eyes. "Thank you for coming," Everly said. "I look forwards to sharing my work with you."

"Your dissertation was an *interesting* read," Dr. Caruso responded. Without waiting for Everly's reply, the woman let herself into the conference room, and overtook Dr. Peart on a journey to one of the frontmost seats.

My work is... interesting? Was that sarcastic or sincere? Everly pondered, turning to face her next guests while feeling a little frazzled by that interaction.

"Interesting is good!" Everly's mother cheered, reading the young scholar's mind like a book. Her father nodded in agreement.

"Hey, you two. Thank you for coming," Everly cheered, ushering her two parents into the room. "I think you're the last group. I'll call down the stairs for Niko, and then we'll get started soon."

"I'm so proud of you!" Everly's mother cheered, pulling her into a hug.

"Good luck," Everly's father added, patting the small of Everly's back.

Everly reciprocated the loving gestures, then sent her parents to their seats.

With everyone set to get started, Everly hustled over to the marble staircase, and called down to the bottom. "I think that's everyone, Niko! You can come up."

"Sounds good! I'll head up!" a voice replied from down below. Soon after, the sound of the research center's main entrance shutting closed reverberated up the staircase.

Everly turned back to face the conference room. *This is really it,* she mused. As she took a deep breath, the sensation of an imaginary string unfurled, tugging down on her right eyelid.

Once again, Everly tilted her head slightly to the left, and began to blink in a rhythmic pattern. *This stupid string reminds me of the nightmare I had last night,* Everly recalled. *I hope my defense goes better this time.*

Everly sighed, listening to Niko's footsteps echo as he climbed up to the second floor.

"How's my hair?" Everly asked as soon as Niko came into view.

"You look fine," Niko replied. "Ready?"

Everly nodded. "Ready as I'll ever be."

7 | SPOTLIGHT

"The foundational unit of machine learning is the neural network," Everly explained. She stood at the front of the conference room, facing out towards her audience of friends, family, peers, and professors.

Everly looked down at a short black remote in her hand. She clicked it, and felt the light change behind her, as her projected presentation shifted to a slide with some bullet points.

"Inside neural networks are groups of numbers called *weights*," she continued. "These weights define the internal algorithm that's ultimately run when you feed input data to a neural network. The weights start out as random numbers, but if we have some input data with a known output that we deem desirable, then we can adjust the weights so they're slightly closer to an algorithm that would, given the input, yield the desired output. Give a large dataset of inputs and desired outputs, you can repeat that adjustment thousands of times, until your neural network can consistently estimate a good answer for whatever input data you were training it to handle."

"This is a really cool idea," Everly summarized. "By adjusting the weights of a neural network, we can effectively train it estimate a solution for any problem."

The young scholar clicked her remote once more, and the presentation displayed an image of thousands of numbers. The slide was titled: "*An Image of the Weights of a Trained Neural Network.*"

"When I first came to this university, I wanted to learn more about what these weights were actually doing," Everly explained. "I know that they're estimating the answer for a task they were trained to do, and I know mathematically how the linear algebra concepts work to make that happen, but there's a layer of explainability that's lost when a computer does these calculations for you. So, I started training some neural networks on different tasks, then did the process of feeding data through their trained weights with pen and paper."

Everly clicked to her next slide, which displayed photographs of the dozens of notebooks she'd filled with mathematical calculations: sending data through neural networks by hand, rather than with computer code.

"Through this exploration, I found something interesting," Everly continued. "Often, there's repetition within these weights. To be clear, the numbers which make up the weights themselves are different from one another. However, the *work* that they're doing—how they're actually interacting with input data, to estimate an answer for different parts of a problem—can sometimes have a lot of overlap."

She clicked to her next slide, which depicted "*An Image of the Weights of a Trained Neural Network*" again. This time, around 20% of the numbers had been grayed out.

"This image, which I showed you before, depicts the weights of an actual neural network that I trained. It was trained to play a very simple video game, where the three inputs describe the location of a ball and some paddles, and a single output describes whether the robot should move their paddle left or right to hit the ball," Everly revealed. "You'll notice, with this version of the diagram, I've deleted a fair amount of the weights."

She then clicked to her next slide, depicting two animations of a robot playing a video game. "The weights that I removed, were just doing duplicate work that other weights could do well enough on their own," Everly explained. "In these two animations, you can see a robot playing a video game. On the left, the robot's taking actions based on calculations from the full neural network. On the right, the robot is using the modified neural network to make decisions—the neural network with about 20% of the weights removed. Even with all those weights missing, the robot on the right is only about 2% worse at the video game than the original robot."

Everly clicked her remote again, displaying the weights of the modified neural network again. "So, that's interesting... now, let's take it a step further. If the removed weights are doing nothing, instead of turning them off, let's see if we can redirect their attention to something else," she continued. "Instead of turning those weights off, I replaced them with random numbers, and then started training *even more*. The result?"

She clicked her remote once more, revealing a new duo of animations. The robot on the right side was clearly better at the video game than the robot on the left side. "I let *both* robots continue training from the point where they left off. However, while the robot on the left side continued training on top of the *original* neural network, the robot on the right side only got to keep the roughly 80% of weights that were deemed useful, and had to effectively *redo* training on the other 20% of weights that were deemed repetitive and had been changed back to random numbers."

"As you can see, the robot on the right side is much better at the game," Everly pointed out. "This is because its neural network was able to use those weights that we reset, to explore new computational pathways. Meanwhile, the robot on the left side was stuck trying to optimize the paths it had already chosen—which included all those repetitive calculations."

Everly clicked to another slide, which displayed a picture of her first published research paper. "This is the discovery encapsulated by my first paper, *Repetitive Behavior Intervention for Neural Networks*. Following that, we built up a refined methodology to leverage this discovery for improving neural network training."

Everly clicked again, revealing three more research publications, each with her name listed as the primary author. "For our first improvement, we designed a robust algorithm to *automatically* analyze neural networks *while* they're being trained, to identify those repetitive calculations as they come up," Everly explained. "Then, with our next paper, we defined a method to redirect those repetitive computations as *soon* as they were detected. Rather than resetting them to random numbers like we did in my first paper, we instead very intentionally nudged them towards unexplored computational pathways. This allowed neural networks to consistently perform better on a variety of machine learning problems. After that, we published a paper about training our *own* neural network to analyze *other* neural networks, find repetitive calculations in them, and redirect those weights towards novel computational paths—a machine learning approach to doing what we'd done in the earlier papers. This was ultimately able to achieve even better results."

An unnerving feeling suddenly grew in the back of Everly's throat. She felt a wave of embarrassment flood her face and ears, as the insurmountable urge to release an expletive immediately began to build up like a pressurized balloon.

Everly lightly put her left hand over her mouth, ready to physically grip own jaw shut if that's what it came to. Urges to whistle began building alongside the expletive, and the sensation of a tugging string on her right eyelid tightened—threatening to rip out her eye if she didn't jerk her head to the right *immediately.*

Why now? Everly's mind raced, feeling alarmed. Her body flooded with adrenaline as she pondered her options. *A full-blown tic attack, and so early into my presentation? I don't think I can hold back all of these with my CBIT tactics.*

Everly clicked her remote, switching the presentation to the next slide. She watched as the change momentarily distracted her audience—moving their glares off her, and onto the new information being projected at the wall. This was a sweet second of privacy, but not enough to relieve a tic attack.

Thinking quickly, Everly popped open the back of the remote in her right hand. With her thumb, she pushed down on one of the batteries—loosening it and pulling it out slightly. *I'd rather be embarrassed by a clumsy moment that could happen to anyone*, Everly thought, *than by a tic attack right in the middle of my presentation.*

With that, Everly weakened her grip, and let the remote slip from her hand. The plastic device made a clicking sound as it hit the ground, busting open and ejecting the loose battery across the floor.

"Oops, there goes the remote," Everly said matter-of-factly, dropping to her knees. She held her head down while she picked up the remote, and mimed searching for the ejected battery while winking and tilting her head.

FUCK! FUCK! FUCK! I'M GONNA KILL MYSELF! FUCK! Everly mouthed, keeping her whisper so low that it was inaudible to the rest of the room. *Please, let this be over soon*, Everly thought, as her muted voice exploded with unruly words and sentences.

The young researcher shivered as a feeling of relief flooded into her body. The feeling wasn't as potent as it would've been if she'd let the tics out as a scream, but it *was* enough to lower the pressure in her system, so she could continue her defense unimpeded.

After taking a moment to gather herself, Everly let out a deep breath. *Time for an excuse as to why I just spent 10 seconds picking something up off the floor*, she mused.

"Oh, I see it!" Everly said. She stood up, pointing towards the conference table. "Sorry; it looks like the battery somehow flung out of the remote when it hit the ground. It's just under the conference table. Niko—erm, Dr. Velkov—would you mind grabbing it?"

Niko nodded. "Of course," he agreed, kneeling down and feeling around on the floor. The other two council members gave Everly a look of pity.

My face must be red with embarrassment, Everly thought to herself. She quickly adjusted her hair, and wiped her brow. *If they think it's because I dropped my remote on the floor, I'll happily accept their pity.*

"Here you go!" Niko said, leaning over the table to hand Everly back the battery.

"Thank you so much," she replied, accepting the stout battery, and placing it back into the remote.

"Sorry about that," Everly apologized. The young researcher looked up at the slide behind her. "Ah, yes. Where was I?"

Everly took one more deep breath, then restarted her competing responses: she tilted her head slightly left, tightened her diaphragm, and started blinking rhythmically.

"After publishing those four papers, I spent some time working with the Outer Space Exploration Agency, also known as OSEA," Everly continued. She took care to speak matter-of-factly, as if she weren't focused on simultaneously doing three different competing responses while presenting this research.

"By utilizing weights more efficiently as a result of my discoveries, we were able to train smaller neural networks at OSEA for tasks that previously required a larger number of weights," Everly explained. "This application of my research was important for OSEA, because putting any amount of code onto rockets and satellites is expensive—so, they're always looking for ways to lower their memory and computational needs without giving up functionality."

Everly clicked the remote once more, revealing a slide with two research publications. "My work at OSEA led to another paper publication, as did my work a couple years later at a company called AccessibleML," Everly continued. "At AccessibleML, my discovery allowed their enormous neural networks—ones which had reached the ceiling of how much memory and computational power they could spare—to improve further, since they could now upgrade their weights by training more *efficiently* rather than by throwing more physical resources into their projects. With these two additional papers, I've shown that my research has applications beyond academia, as it has already led to advancements in both the government and in private industry."

Everly clicked the remote once more. "With that, we've gotten through the overview," she said. "Next, I'm going to walk your through each of these papers with a more in-depth perspective."

Everly spent the next 30 minutes going through slides which dove deeper into her research. She presented her work clearly and concisely, cutting through complex topics in a way that even less technical audience members could understand. With this method of presenting, that Everly hoped the council members might see promise in the idea of her becoming a professor someday. Additionally, as she presented, Everly kept her tics at bay—she remained vigilant with her competing responses throughout the entire presentation, and fortunately, was not overwhelmed by any more particularly bad tic attacks while she spoke.

"…and I believe that's my time," Everly said as she clicked to the final slide. "To end this off, I will now open the floor to questions from the audience."

All three council members started to speak at once, then stopped to decide amongst themselves who would ask their question first.

Here comes the hard part, Everly mused. She audibly gulped, and as her nerves rose, the imaginary string tugged down on her eyelid with renewed intensity.

8 | QUESTIONS

"Miss Hawthorne, removing weights from neural networks is a bold move," Dr. Peart proclaimed, scratching his wrinkly chin as he spoke. "How did you protect stability of the neural networks while doing that, and how did you validate your approach?"

"I'll start with the validation, since that might answer the other part of your question, too," Everly replied. "We validated the approach, sort of the same way you'd validate any neural network. During training, we implemented occasional validation steps, where we would run a separate set of testing data through the neural network to figure out its accuracy—in our case, getting an accuracy for the model with and without a set of suspected duplicate weights."

A small squeak escaped Everly's throat, but nobody in the room seemed to notice. She tightened her diaphragm further, then continued. "We could then compare the accuracies between the two versions of the model, to validate how significantly things would change by removing a suspected set of duplicate weights. With that, we could protect the model's stability by following through with removing the weights if such removal wouldn't de-stabilize everything."

"How do you envision the scalability of this approach, especially when dealing with larger and more complex neural networks?" Dr. Caruso piped up.

"I feel I've empirically proven that scalability isn't an issue with this method," Everly said. "The algorithm modifies foundational aspects of the neural network, so as shown in some of my earlier papers, it's perfectly feasible to apply it to more complex models—if a model based on some form of neural network, then it can probably gain something from my methodology. In terms of *larger* models, my algorithm can even make it *easier* to do training, by lowering computational needs via removing unnecessary weights—as demonstrated through my work with AccessibleML."

"I'd think it's fair to say that your research has demonstrated significant applications for academia, government work, and industry work," Niko said. "How do you foresee the future development of this line of research?"

Everly visibly relaxed her shoulders, in response to Niko's softball question. "As I mentioned earlier, we've found the most success using a machine learning approach for detecting the duplicate weights," Everly replied. "I'd like to see experimentation with different models, to possibly improve the algorithm further. I'd also like to see how this method can integrate with other emerging technologies, beyond the works at OSEA and AccessibleML."

Everly continued to answer questions for the research committee, with the topics ranging from model explainability to safeguards and ethical considerations. Most of the questions were quite technical—Everly did her best to explain herself well when answering them, while simultaneously keeping her tics at bay.

Once there were only a few minutes left in the Q&A time, the research committee opened things up to the wider audience.

"Any of you, back there, want to ask Miss Hawthorne a question?" Dr. Peart prodded, holding his cane steady against the ground as he swiveled in his seat to look back. "This is your chance."

Everly looked out at the audience. Her parents appeared uncomfortable; they likely felt pressured to ask a question, but fearful that they might mess up their daughter's presentation. Kai, Daniel, and Matt—the three younger computer scientists from Niko's ever-growing research lab—were all staring at one another, as if each daring each other to speak up.

Chelsea, on the other hand, proudly raised her hand from the back of the room. Everly gestured to her best friend, like a teacher calling on a student.

"How did you come up with your research idea?" Chelsea asked.

Everly pondered this question for a moment. *Chelsea doesn't know about my disability*, she mused. *Otherwise, maybe she wouldn't have asked that? Well, I guess... if I answer tactfully, there's no reason not to be truthful. It's kind of a cool story, I suppose.*

"The concept of a neural network was loosely based on the human brain," Everly began. "So, I think studying the human brain is interesting, and can be a place to explore new ideas for furthering this research."

Everly kept her eyes locked on Chelsea as she spoke. She didn't want to look at her parents or Niko while answer this, since they would be aware how closely it danced around a sensitive topic for her.

"There's a relatively rare neurological disease known as Tourette syndrome, where the brain starts doing repetitive actions without consent from the consciousness of that body," Everly explained. "These uninvited actions are called tics. You can think of it sort of like hiccups: a sudden, repetitive, and sometimes frankly odd sound or movement that starts to be produced by the body for no apparent reason."

The act of talking about Tourette syndrome seemed to make the Everly's tic-related sensations more unbearable—she felt herself struggling to keep them at bay. Everly paused, took a deep breath, and let her body relax a bit. After a moment, she restarted her CBIT tactics as if she hadn't felt anything, and kept talking.

"So, when I noticed some repetitive, unnecessary calculations happening in neural networks, it reminded me of that idea of tics coming from the brain," Everly continued. "My first thought was to get rid of the tics, which is why deleting the duplicate weights was the first thing I tried in my first paper."

"Building on that," she continued, holding up a finger to emphasize her point. "There is a method called Cognitive Behavioral Intervention for Tics, or CBIT, where patients with Tourette syndrome are taught how to redirect their body's muscles in a way that prevents repetitive tics from happening. For example, if we were to pretend hiccups are a tic, then you could potentially prevent them by drinking water, holding your breath, clenching your diaphragm, or something—the important thing is, whatever you're doing is intentionally being done by your consciousness, and physically prevents the tics from happening. You can't hiccup and keep your diaphragm tightened at the same time, for example, because both actions require use of your diaphragm."

As she was speaking, Everly was secretly keeping her own diaphragm tightened, to prevent her body from letting out vocal tics between her words. "That is what inspired the original redirection algorithm, and the name of my first paper: *Repetitive Behavior Intervention for Neural Networks*. Like tics, I noticed some repetitive, unnecessary calculations in neural networks. To remove those, we re-trained them—effectively re-directing those calculations to another task."

Everly clicked through some appendix slides on her presentation—where she'd stored some additional graphs, images, pictures, etc. for the Q&A phase of her dissertation—until she arrived at a slide showing a list of her research publications. "Later on, I created a new algorithm to very intentionally re-direct these repetitive weights down new computational pathways. The weights can't do repetitive calculations, and do a different new calculation, at the same time—just like a person's muscles can't do a tic, and a CBIT response, at the same time."

Everly took another deep breath, relaxed her body, then re-started her CBIT tactics again. "That's the big thing that inspired this research. At the beginning, at least."

Chelsea nodded, looking impressed by Everly's long-winded answer.

"How did you learn so much about Tourette syndrome?" Dr. Caruso asked, tilting her head.

"She said that at the start of her answer," Niko piped up. "Studying the human brain is interesting, especially for a person doing research in artificial intelligence. I also like to study neurology in my free time."

"That CBIT stuff sounded more like psychology than neurology, no?" Dr. Caruso countered.

"Or psychotherapy?" Dr. Peart said. Dr. Caruso raised her eyebrow at the old man, and he shrugged.

"I think we're getting a little off topic here," Niko interjected. "Does anyone have more questions about Everly's research?"

"From my OT and my doctor," Everly said. The research committee looked at her quizzically.

Fuck it, Everly thought. *We're all adults here.*

"I'm answering the question," Everly clarified. "Dr. Caruso asked how I learned so much about Tourette syndrome. I learned about it from my OT and my doctor, because I have Tourette syndrome."

"You don't have to share anything you don't want to—" Niko started, but Everly gestured to him that it was okay.

"I've had it since I was 8 years old. CBIT is the only reason that I can be in front of you right now, and appear as if I don't have Tourette syndrome. CBIT tactics are extremely useful, and on my mind frequently—thus, they naturally came to mind while I was studying for my degree, and made their way into inspiring some of my research.

Everly kept her CBIT tactics active, too embarrassed to allow any of her tics through now that the whole audience was aware her condition. Nevertheless, some sense of relief—and not the physical, letting-a-tic-loose sort of relief, but a legitimate releasing-a-mental-burden relief—washed over her. For this small audience of 9 people, she had stopped hiding something that had been weighing on her each minute of every day.

Everly glanced at a ticking clock on the wall of the conference room. "It's 3:01pm," she announced. "I think we're supposed to end roughly around 3pm, right? Are there... any other questions?"

Everly felt blood rushing to her face, as she pondered what she'd just done.

"Uh... I think no. I think we're good?" Niko replied, looking at his peers for confirmation. Dr. Peart and Dr. Caruso nodded in agreement.

"Yep, we will call it here, then," Niko said. "At this time, I would like to invite our speaker and our audience to head back to the lobby of this building. The research committee will remain in this room to discuss the dissertation, and then we will call you all back in once we've come to a decision."

With that, the audience shuffled out of the conference space, with Everly following behind. She could feel her face turning beat red as she walked. Niko hopped out of his chair, and accompanied his most senior student on her way out of the room.

"Excellent work," Niko whispered, as he led Everly out, then closed the door shut behind her.

As her parents ambushed her with a hug, Everly watched her best friend and fellow students descended the marble staircase, towards the lobby.

They all know! she thought with horror. *And now, I have to go sit in the lobby with all of them. What was I thinking?!*

9 | AFTERMATH

"You did so well, honey!" Everly's mother cheered, as she squeezed her daughter close to her chest.

"No matter how their decision turns out, we're very proud of you," her father added.

Everly hugged her parents tight, while watching her friends and fellow students trot down the marble staircase behind them. Although she was nervous to follow them, and potentially hear what they had to say about her—it made her *more* uncomfortable to stay near the conference room, since Niko had asked her to head to the lobby.

"I don't want to accidentally overhear them talking about me," Everly told her parents. "Let's head downstairs."

Everly felt the pitter-patter of butterflies fluttering in her stomach as her hand grazed the cool railing of the marble staircase. As her shoes click-clacked down the steps, she glanced back at her parents. Their faces beamed with pride.

"Hey Chels," Everly called out, turning back to face her friend, and speeding down the steps to catch up with her.

"Evie! That was good stuff!" Chelsea praised as her friend caught up with her. "I didn't know that... uh, thing about you, with the Tourette's—hey, are you okay? Your face just turned super red. Are you nervous about the committee? You've got Niko rooting for you up there; I'm sure it'll be fine!"

"No, I mean yes, I am nervous about that," Everly admitted, "however, more so—could you kind of, keep the Tourette syndrome thing on the low-down? I'm super embarrassed about it. That's why I've never told you. I'm not— well, what I did today was new for me. I'm not ready to just go public about that everywhere, though. So, please don't tell anybody."

Chelsea mimed zipping up her lips, locking them at the edge, and tossing away the key.

"Sure. My lips are sealed!" she agreed. Chelsea then grabbed Everly in a warm embrace, and hopped with excitement. The sudden motion knocked Everly off her feet, causing both women to tumble down the last couple steps of the staircase. From behind them, Everly's mother gasped at the sight.

"Ah! Are you okay?!" Chelsea asked, regaining her footing on solid ground.

"Yes, your purse broke my fall," Everly replied. "Chels! Don't grab people on the stairs like that!" she continued, breaking into a fit of laughter.

"I'm sorrrrryyy!" Chelsea replied. "I'm just so excited for you! Your dissertation looked like it went super well!"

Everly's mother rushed to the bottom of the stairs, and helped Everly get back on her feet.

"Thanks mom," Everly said. The young researcher then scanned the lobby. The three boys from Niko's research lab had conglomerated at a bench near the front, and appeared to be playing games on their phones. They seemed unfazed by Everly's revelation in the conference room.

I think my secret is safe, Everly concluded. *I'll bet those three were barely paying attention, and I know Chelsea would endure torture before giving away something told to her in confidence.*

Everly let out a long, slow sigh—which was cut short, as Chelsea wrapped her friend in another embrace.

"Thanks, guys," Everly said, looking upon her friend and family. "Today was a big step for me. I appreciate you being here."

Everly's father nodded in acknowledgement. "Why don't you three take a seat?" he suggested. "I saw a vending machine in this area when we first came in. I'll buy some snacks and waters for all of us."

"That would be great," Everly said. "Thank you."

As the young researcher sat down between her mother and close friend, she felt tears welling up in her eyes.

"Are you crying?" Chelsea whispered, noticing immediately. "Are those tears of sadness? Joy? Anxiety? Relief?"

"All of the above," Everly replied.

Chelsea and Everly's mother hugged the young researcher from both sides.

"A lot of things happened in that room," Everly continued. "…I'm glad that I did all of them. Now, we just have to wait, and see what the research committee thinks of me."

10 | DECISION

After a period of 15 minutes that felt like hours, Niko called down the stairs.

"We're ready!" he announced. "We'd like to invite all of you back up, and into the conference room."

Everly started to let out a soft whistle, but cut it off by tapping her tongue to the roof of her mouth.

"Welp, it's time," she muttered.

Chelsea and Everly's mother squeezed the young researcher with another hug from both sides, then the group proceeded up the cool stairs, with Everly's father and Niko's other three students following in tow.

Upon reaching the top, they found Niko holding open the doors to the conference room, and ushering them inside. The middle-aged professor made eye contact with Everly, and gave her a friendly smile—but there was a blankness behind facial expression, as if his true intentions were hidden.

I don't know if he's afraid of spoiling some good news or terrified to tell me some bad news, Everly pondered, *but I've known him long enough to be able to tell when there's something he's desperate to share with me.*

Everly entered the conference room with her entourage of friends, family, and peers following closely behind. She took in a deep breath, then felt a tug on her right eyelid—forcing her head to tilt to the right, her right eye to wink, and a crick to form in her right shoulder.

As a new whistle started building up in her throat, Everly took in another deep breath, then exhaled slowly. As she stepped closer and closer to the front of the room, she tilted her head to the left, combatting the tugging sensation that pulled her to the right. She also began to blink rhythmically, though a thin veil of tears welling up her eyes.

Everly cracked her right shoulder as she stepped behind the small wooden podium at the front of the room.

"I'd like to thank the committee for examining my dissertation," she said, careful to keep her tongue glued to the roof of her mouth between words—lest she allow a whistle to escape through her lips. "I look forward to hearing your feedback and your decision."

Mentally, Everly felt relief after speaking those words— now, all she had to do, was stand at the front of the room and listen. Physically, however, every muscle in her body was tensed, and she could feel the chemical-like flow of adrenaline rushing through her system.

Niko returned to his seat in the middle of the council. His face, previously a juxtaposition of warmth and blankness, now showed excitement.

I think that's a good sign, Everly thought.

"I'm going to talk first," Niko announced. "We're supposed to do this whole thing, where each member of the committee says something nice, and then I do the reveal at the end, but I can't wait that long."

Niko locked eyes with Everly, and his face broke into a silly grin. "Everly, you were my first student. You have impressed me every year that you've been here. Your work has always been robust, carefully thought-through, and highly accurate. Your paper writing has also been some of the highest quality work I've seen. I can't wait to see more. It has been an honor to work with you, Dr. Hawthorne."

The phrase "Dr. Hawthorne" shot through Everly like a jolt of happy lightning.

"*Bitch!*" Everly's body whispered, incited by the excitement. Everly immediately covered her mouth with her hand to stifle any further outbursts. As was her habit, she did this in a way that looked natural—as if she was just hiding her smile at the good news, and as if her whispered outburst was just an odd-sounding cough. As such, nobody in the room seemed to notice—even though they were all aware of her condition now.

"Well, the cat's out of the bag, but we're still going to share our thoughts," Dr. Peart said. "I learned lots of new things from your presentation today, Dr. Hawthorne, and that's the kind of thing that keeps me coming into this building every morning. I'd like to thank you for sharing your findings, and I, too, am looking forward to seeing what you come up with next."

Everly nodded with thanks at Dr. Peart, acknowledging his kind words. As she did, Dr. Caruso cleared her throat, picked up a sheet of paper she'd written on, and adjusted her glasses.

"By applying principles you learned from managing your Tourette syndrome, you were able to transform your personal experiences into a technical advantage for your research," Dr. Caruso praised. "That is an incredible strength. This committee hopes you will continue to embrace your uniqueness as you further explore bridging the gap between human experiences and artificial intelligence advancements. We hope to aid you with that exploration, by telling you this today— then I gesture to Niko, but he already said it, so I'll just say it again—you've passed, with no revisions. Congratulations, Dr. Hawthorne."

"Congratulations, Dr. Hawthorne," Niko and Dr. Peart repeated. The three committee members then stood up from their chairs, and joined Everly on the stage, to each give her a congratulatory handshake and pat on the back.

Everly smiled, as a wave of relief and joy flowed through her system. *Dr. Hawthorne!* she mused. *Now that has a nice ring to it!*

Epilogue | AUTHENTICITY

Ten years ago today, I received my PhD in computer science, mused a middle-aged Everly as she stared at the achievement displayed upon her office wall. She was staring at a copy of it, of course; her real PhD was sitting in a safe, back home.

Everly glanced along the wall of her office. Her eyes grazed past a sign with the definition of Tourette syndrome, which hung amongst numerous machine learning diagrams, framed publications, and a collection of interesting maps.

As her eyes landed upon her desktop computer, she smirked. *The other professors say I shouldn't obsess over that one website, but today's a special day*, she thought. *Plus, we just finished the winter semester, so there's probably some new reviews.*

As Dr. Hawthorne made her way to her desk chair, she felt the sensation of invisible springs along her fingertips. These imaginary springs oscillated, pulling her fingers to her palms suddenly, then releasing them. This forced both of her hands to do sort of a one-handed clap, over and over.

Absent-mindedly, Everly interlaced her fingers together, stopping the one-handed clapping tic. After she sat down, she paused for a minute, allowing the tic's sensations to subside.

Once she was ready, Everly clicked her mouse, and logged in with her old student email. Upon clicking 'Submit,' the computer rejected her login, stating that the email was no longer valid.

Ah! she thought, slapping a hand to her forehead. *Ten years later, and I'm still making that mistake!*

Everly deleted her old student email, and replaced it with her faculty email for the same university. This time, when she clicked 'Submit,' the computer proceeded successfully.

Everly opened her browser and navigated to a popular website where college students leave reviews of their professors. The website was famous for using these reviews to rank professors at a university based on student opinions.

Everly searched the name of her university, then sorted the professors by highest number of positive reviews. Near the top, sat the name "Dr. Everly Hawthorne"—one step higher in the rankings than the ever-popular Dr. Niko Velkov.

First place! Everly thought, clapping her hands together gleefully. *I finally kicked Niko down from his throne! I can't wait to tell him.*

Everly clicked on her name, then sorted the reviews by most recent. She clicked on the first review she saw, and read through it.

Review of Professor Hawthorne

- Teaching Quality: 10/10
- Communication Skills: 10/10
- Approachability: 10/10
- Availability: 9/10
- Clarity of Expectations: 10/10

Comments:

Everyone knows Hawthorne is a fantastic professor, but for me, the approachability is where she really shines (I would give an 11/10 for that category if I could).

She starts each semester by informing the students about her Tourette syndrome, and explaining how she hides it (I wouldn't have ever noticed it if she hadn't told us about it).

Then, she tells a story about how her first research publication was inspired by her experiences with that condition.

She ends the story by saying that we're all welcome here, and regardless of whatever we may be dealing with (even something that isn't obvious, like the condition in her story), that every part of our background makes us more complicated, unique, and smart individuals. I'm paraphrasing (she says it better than I can think to type it), but that's the gist. That was a really meaningful/eye-opening moment for me.

For context, I have ADHD, and I do not tell people about it. I work very hard to keep it hidden, because I'm very embarrassed about it, and I don't want to introduce a bias in professors grading me, students befriending me, employers interviewing me, etc.

I'm not quite at the level where I feel ready to talk openly about my ADHD yet, but I wanted to say that I feel very welcomed in Hawthorne's class, and I am absolutely going to take more classes with her in the future!!

~~~

Everly smiled. Her eyes had watered up a little from reading the kind review, so she grabbed a tissue and wiped them clean.

That's exactly what I'm going for! she thought to herself. Then, Everly frowned. *What's up with the 9/10 on availability, though? Should I be scheduling more office hours?*

She clicked open her calendar, and added some additional office hours for the upcoming spring semester. She also wrote "Check emails more frequently" on a sticky note, and attached it to her computer monitor.

Alright, time to read some more, she mused with a smile. Everly exited the review she'd just read, and clicked open the next one.

This is heaven, she thought, as her eyes began scanning the next set of comments. *I'm so happy to be who I am!*